MY DAD IS BRILLIANT

Nick Butterworth

WALKER BOOKS

AND SUBSIDIARIES

LONDON · BOSTON · SYDNEY · AUCKLAND

My dad is
brilliant.

THIS WALKER BOOK BELONGS TO:

_____

_____

_____

First published 1989 by Walker Books Ltd
87 Vauxhall Walk, London SE11 5HJ

This edition published 2001

4 6 8 10 9 7 5

© 1989 Nick Butterworth

The right of Nick Butterworth to be identified as
author/illustrator of this work has been asserted
by him in accordance with the Copyright, Designs
and Patents Act 1988

This book has been typeset in Times

Printed in China

British Library Cataloguing in Publication Data:
a catalogue record for this book is available from the British Library

ISBN 0-7445-8248-2

www.walkerbooks.co.uk

He's as
strong as a
gorilla …

and he can
run like a
cheetah …

and he can
play any
instrument …

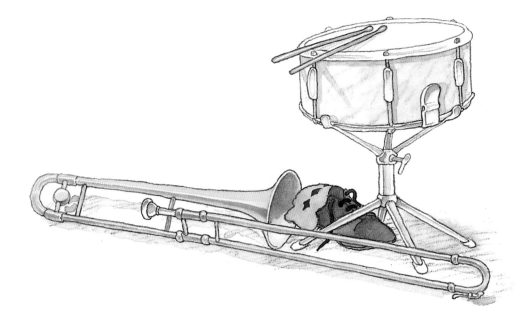

and he's
a marvellous
cook …

and he's
fantastic on
roller skates...

and he's
brilliant at making
things ...

and he can
sing like a
pop star ...

and he can
juggle with
anything ...

and he's not
a bit frightened
of the dark …

and he tells the
funniest jokes
in the world.

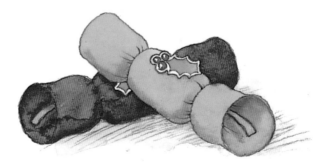

It's great to
have a dad
like mine.

It's brilliant!

WALKER BOOKS is the world's leading
independent publisher of children's books.
Working with the best authors and illustrators
we create books for all ages, from babies
to teenagers – books your child will
grow up with and always remember. So…

FOR THE BEST CHILDREN'S BOOKS,
LOOK FOR THE BEAR